This book belongs to:

Wyatt David Veldkamp

Love Grandpa & Grandma

"2023"   Blessings

A Treasury of
Christmas
Stories &
Songs

First published 2016 by Parragon Books, Ltd.

Copyright © 2023 Cottage Door Press, LLC.
5005 Newport Drive
Rolling Meadows, Illinois 60008

Cover and additional illustrations by Claire McElfatrick
Virginia O'Hanlon. Letter to the editor, *The Sun*, September 21, 1897.
Francis P. Church. "Is There a Santa Claus?," *The Sun*, September 21, 1897.
Clement C. Moore. "A Visit from St. Nicholas," *The Sentinel*, December 23, 1823.
Song illustrations by Jenny Løvlie, Claire McElfatrick,
Hannah Tolson, and Rosie Wheeldon

ISBN: 978-1-64638-502-7

Parragon Books is an imprint of Cottage Door Press, LLC.
Parragon® and the Parragon® logo are registered trademarks of
Cottage Door Press, LLC.

A Treasury of
Christmas
Stories &
Songs

PaRragon®

Table of Contents

The First Christmas

Written by Lucy Cuthew
Illustrated by Jenny Løvlie

Many years ago, a couple, named Mary and Joseph were engaged to be married. They lived in the town of Nazareth, in Galilee.

They were not rich, but they were good, kind people who worked hard, and cared for one another.

One day, the angel Gabriel appeared
to Mary. "Do not be afraid," said Gabriel.
"I have a message from God."

Mary felt blessed to be visited by an
angel, but she wondered what message
the angel could have for her.

"Mary," said Gabriel. "You are special to God. You will give birth to a child who will bring peace and hope to all the world. He will be the Savior of humankind."

Mary was afraid as she listened to the angel, for she wondered how this message could be true. But she decided to talk to Joseph.

When Mary told Joseph, he was confused and frightened, too. How could it be that the son of God would be born to them?

That night as he slept, he had a strange yet peaceful dream. In the dream, the angel Gabriel came to him.

"Joseph," said Gabriel, "what Mary tells you is true. The child she carries is the son of God. You will name him Jesus, which means Savior, for he will save his people from their sins."

So Joseph and Mary married, and they waited happily for the baby to arrive.

Just before the baby was due to be born, the emperor ordered everyone to go back to the town of their birth. He wanted to count how many people lived in different parts of the Roman Empire.

Joseph was a descendant of King David of Judea, so he and Mary had to travel all the way from Nazareth to Bethlehem.

The journey would be long and hard, especially because Mary was about to have her baby.

When they reached Bethlehem, Mary and Joseph had to find somewhere to stay. However, as they went wearily from door to door, they found that there were so many other travelers that there was not even one place with a room for them.

The sun set and the stars were out. Mary could feel that the baby would arrive soon.

Finally, an innkeeper took pity on them. Although he had no room inside, he offered Mary and Joseph his stable.

Mary and Joseph joined the animals in the humble stable. They had a roof over their heads, soft bedding to rest on, and they had one another.

The warm breath of the sleeping animals filled the hay-scented air. The stars shone in the night sky. Soon, Mary's baby was born.

There was no crib to place him in, but there was a little manger. Joseph filled it with soft straw, and Mary wrapped the baby in cloth and laid him in the manger to sleep.

Meanwhile, in the fields, a group of shepherds were watching over their flocks of sheep. As they looked up at the starry sky, an angel appeared, surrounded by blazing light.

"Do not be afraid," said the angel. "I have good news! Your Savior was born this very night, Christ the Lord! You will find him in Bethlehem. He is in a humble stable, wrapped in cloth and sleeping in a manger."

The shepherds were amazed.

Then a choir of angels appeared in the sky, singing with the sweetest voices the shepherds had ever heard.

"Glory to God in the highest!" the angels sang. "Peace and goodwill to all on Earth."

The light of the angels shone down upon the awestruck shepherds.

They were so moved by the beauty of the song that they decided to go to Bethlehem and see this special baby for themselves.

When the shepherds reached the stable in Bethlehem,
they found everything was just as the angel had told them.
There lay a baby, wrapped in cloth, sleeping in a manger.

"The Savior has been born!" they cried. "Praise the Lord."

They told Mary how the angels guided them.

Mary was amazed that angels had visited these shepherds
to tell them of the birth of her son.

In the East, three wise kings had spent many
years waiting for a savior promised by God.
　　The night that Mary's baby was born,
they saw a star brighter than any they had
ever seen before.
　　They took it as a sign, and they followed
the star, carrying precious gifts of gold,
frankincense, and myrrh.

The bright star led the kings to the stable where Mary, Joseph, and Jesus were resting.

When the kings saw the baby, they knelt down and worshipped him.

Each king presented his gift to the little child in turn. The first gave him gold, which shone as brightly as the star in the sky. The second gave frankincense, a rare fragrance. The third gave myrrh, which was used for healing.

These precious gifts were the very first gifts of Christmas.

That starry night, in a humble stable, Jesus Christ had been born. And on that very first Christmas night, all those who gathered worshipped him as the bringer of peace, hope, and joy to all the world.

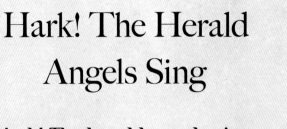

Hark! The Herald Angels Sing

Hark! The herald angels sing,
Glory to the newborn king!
Peace on earth, and mercy mild;
God and sinners reconciled!
Joyful, all ye nations rise.
Join the triumph of the skies.
With th'angelic host proclaim,
Christ is born in Bethlehem!
Hark, the herald angels sing,
Glory to the newborn king!

O Come, All Ye Faithful

O come, all ye faithful,
Joyful and triumphant!
O come ye, O come ye to Bethlehem.
Come and behold him,
Born the King of angels;

O come, let us adore him,
O come, let us adore him,
O come, let us adore him,
Christ the Lord!

The Nutcracker

Based on the story by E.T.A. Hoffmann
Illustrated by Valeria Docampo

It was Christmas Eve and the snow was falling gently. Clara and her brother, Fritz, were very excited. That night, there would be a magnificent party with music and dancing, as well as lots of fantastic presents!

Fritz was busy with his toy soldiers, lining them up and giving them their orders.

Clara put the finishing touches on their enormous tree. She hung shining ornaments and candy canes tied with bows from the branches.

"This is my favorite part," Clara said to her brother as she lifted up a beautiful fairy with delicate wings and a sugarplum-colored dress.

At last, it was time for the
party to begin.

"The guests are arriving!"
cried Clara, peering out of her
bedroom window.

Fritz ran over to see who was
crunching through the snow.

"Can you see Godfather
Drosselmeyer?" asked Clara.

"Yes, there he is waving!"
cried Fritz. "Come on!"

Their godfather was a famous
toymaker. He made the most
magical toys in the whole city.
Clara and Fritz could hardly wait to
see what he had brought for them.

Godfather Drosselmeyer hugged the children at the door, and with a flourish, produced two gifts.

Fritz eagerly unwrapped a box of toy soldiers. For Clara, there was a wooden nutcracker in the shape of a soldier.

"Take good care of him," said Godfather Drosselmeyer. "He is very special."

"I love him," Clara whispered.

"Thank you."

"But he's a soldier," said Fritz. "He should be mine."

"You can't have him!" cried Clara.

Fritz tried to snatch the Nutcracker away
from her. He pulled and Clara tugged, and then ...

CRACK!

The Nutcracker's leg snapped off!

Clara cradled the Nutcracker in her arms and wept.

"Don't cry, Clara," said her godfather gently. "This soldier has been wounded, but I can soon fix him."

Godfather Drosselmeyer pulled a little tool pouch from his pocket and quickly mended the Nutcracker, so that he looked as good as new.

"Oh, thank you," said Clara, drying her eyes. "I'll never let anyone hurt him again."

Everyone was dancing now and the house was filled with music and laughter. Clara placed the Nutcracker carefully under the Christmas tree and joined the party.

Finally, the last dance was danced, and the guests said their goodbyes. The family went to bed, and the house was dark and quiet.

Clara awoke to hear the last bong of the clock striking midnight.

"Oh no!" she thought. "I left the Nutcracker all alone under the tree."

Clara tiptoed downstairs and crept under the Christmas tree, holding the Nutcracker protectively.

Suddenly, the tree started to grow taller and taller! Or was it just that Clara was shrinking?

"What's happening?" she cried.

"Don't be afraid," said a kind voice.
Clara turned around. Her Nutcracker had come
alive! Behind him, Fritz's soldiers were sitting
up in their toy box, and Clara's dolls were
gazing around.

Before Clara could speak, she heard a scurrying sound, and from
every nook and cranny, an army of mice poured into the room!
They were led by a giant Mouse King with a golden crown.

"ATTACK!" he squealed.

"Who will fight with me?" cried the Nutcracker. The soldiers
marched boldly out of the toy box.

"TO BATTLE!" ordered the Nutcracker.
The soldiers shouted and cheered, and the
mice squealed and squeaked.

Suddenly, Clara saw the Mouse King spring toward her beloved Nutcracker, baring his teeth.

"No!' cried Clara. She snatched off her slipper and hurled it at the Mouse King. He fell to the ground with a cry, and his crown tumbled from his head.

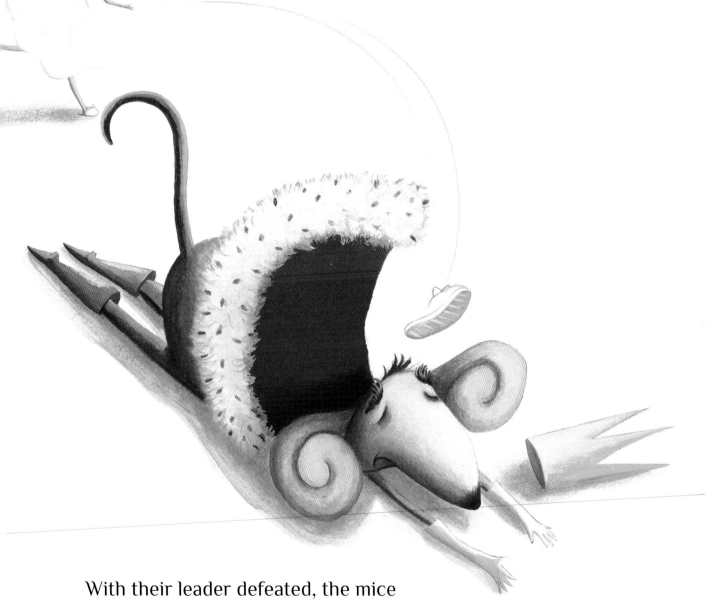

With their leader defeated, the mice scurried away in fear. The battle was won!

The Nutcracker picked up Clara's
slipper and placed it on her foot. She
gasped — the Nutcracker had transformed
into a handsome prince!

"I owe you my life, Princess Clara," he said.
"You broke the spell that was put on me long
ago by a wicked Mouse Queen."

"I'm glad that you're safe," said Clara.
"But you are mistaken — I'm not a princess."

"Are you sure?" asked the Prince.

Clara looked down and saw that she was
wearing a glittering gown and satin shoes!

"Come," said the Prince. "I am going to
take you on a wonderful adventure."

The walls of the living room seemed to fade away, and a beautiful sleigh drew up in front of them, led by two reindeer.

Clara and the Prince climbed aboard, and they were swept high into the sky among the sparkling stars.

Suddenly, Clara caught sight of a magical land down below. Lollipop trees shimmered on cotton candy hills. There were gingerbread houses, rivers of honey, and an orange-scented breeze.

"Where are we?" gasped Clara.

"This is the Kingdom of Sweets," said the Prince.

The sleigh landed beside a rose-colored lake and changed into a sea chariot pulled by dolphins. Swans swam beside them, and shimmering fish leapt out of the water.

On the far side of the lake was a magnificent marzipan palace.
A fairy with delicate wings was waving to them from the gate.

"Look," said the Prince. "It's the Sugarplum Fairy!"

"Prince Nutcracker!" cried the fairy. "You are home at last."

"This is Princess Clara," said the Prince, as they stepped
ashore. "She saved my life and broke the Mouse Queen's spell."

The Sugarplum Fairy hugged Clara.

"Come and join the celebration!" she said.

Inside the palace, Clara and the Prince feasted on delicious cakes and sweets.

They watched in wonder as dancers from every corner of the world whirled around the room.

Then it was the Sugarplum Fairy's turn. Clara had never seen such dancing! She twirled and twirled until all Clara could see was the blur of her plum-colored dress.

Clara's eyelids began to droop. Her adventures had made her tired. The sound of the music became fainter and fainter...

When Clara woke on Christmas morning,
she found herself curled up under the Christmas
tree next to the Nutcracker. Toys were strewn across
the floor, and her parents were standing over her.

"What have you been doing?" asked her father.

"Oh, I've had the most wonderful
adventure," said Clara.

She told her parents all about the
Mouse King, the Nutcracker Prince,
and the Kingdom of Sweets.

"It was just a dream, darling," said her mother.

Clara gazed up at the sugarplum-colored fairy on top
of the tree. Then she looked at the wooden Nutcracker
in her hands.

"Perhaps it was," she said.

Clara noticed something glinting on the carpet,
and a smile spread across her face. It was a tiny
golden crown!

"Merry Christmas, Prince
Nutcracker," she whispered.

Away in a Manger

Away in a manger, no crib for a bed,
The little Lord Jesus lay down his sweet head.
The stars in the bright sky looked down where he lay,
The little Lord Jesus asleep on the hay.

The cattle are lowing, the poor baby wakes.
But little Lord Jesus, no crying he makes.
I love thee, Lord Jesus; look down from the sky,
And stay my cradle till morning is nigh.

Be near me, Lord Jesus, I ask thee to stay
Close by me forever, and love me, I pray.
Bless all the dear children in thy tender care,
And take us to heaven, to live with thee there.

O Christmas Tree

O Christmas tree, O Christmas tree,
Thy leaves are so unchanging.
Not only green when summer's here,
But also when it's cold and drear.
O Christmas tree, O Christmas tree,
Thy leaves are so unchanging.

A Christmas Carol

Adapted by Lucy Cuthew
from the original by Charles Dickens
Illustrated by Dinara Mirtalipova

It was a snowy Christmas Eve morning and Ebenezer Scrooge was waiting for his clerk, Bob Cratchit, to arrive for work.

"You're late!" said Scrooge, when Bob appeared less than a minute after nine o'clock.

"I am sorry, sir," said Bob. "I had to look after my son. He is not well—"

"No excuses!" said Scrooge. "Now get to work before I change my mind about letting you have tomorrow off."

Bob's heart sank. Tomorrow was
Christmas, and he was hoping to spend
it with his family.

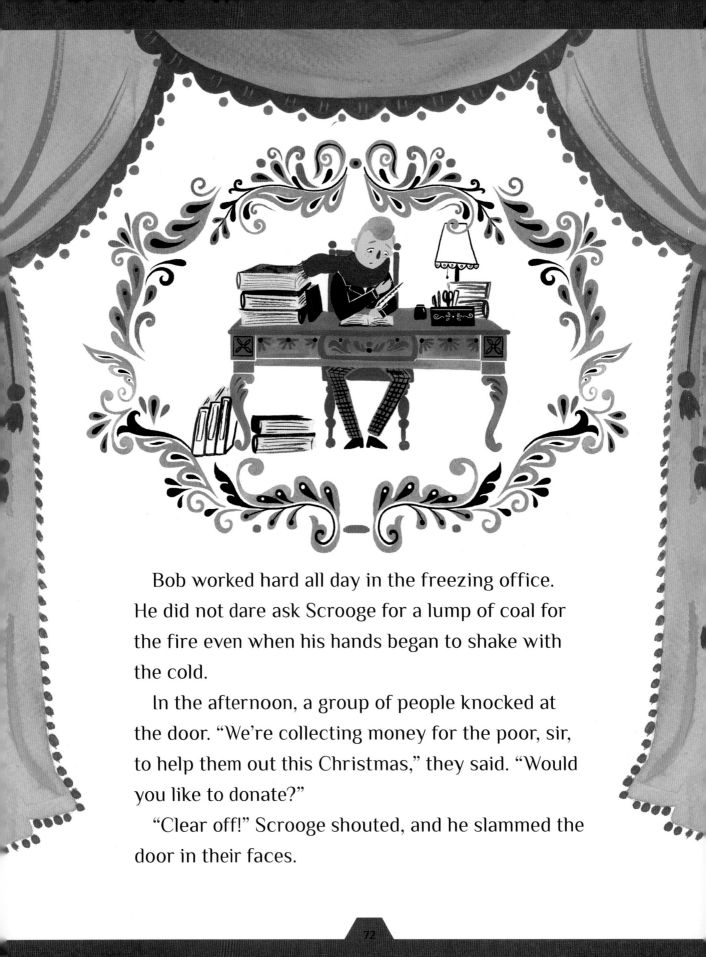

Bob worked hard all day in the freezing office. He did not dare ask Scrooge for a lump of coal for the fire even when his hands began to shake with the cold.

In the afternoon, a group of people knocked at the door. "We're collecting money for the poor, sir, to help them out this Christmas," they said. "Would you like to donate?"

"Clear off!" Scrooge shouted, and he slammed the door in their faces.

A little later Scrooge's cheerful nephew, Fred, arrived.

"Happy Christmas, Uncle!" he said warmly, and invited Scrooge for Christmas dinner.

"Bah, humbug!" Scrooge declared. "What is so happy about Christmas?" He would rather spend the day counting his money than in the company of Fred and his family.

That night, Scrooge woke
in the darkness to the chime of
church bells.

As the clock struck two, a ghost appeared
at the end of his bed, dressed in a long, white gown.
Scrooge pulled the covers around him in fright.

"Ebenezer Scrooge," said the spirit. "You must change your
ways or be miserable until the end of time. Tonight three
spirits will visit you to show you how things have been,
how they are, and how they might be. I am the first."

"Heavens!" cried Scrooge. "Spirit, please leave me!"

But the ghost rose into the air and then,
laying a hand on Scrooge's heart, lifted him, too.

"I am the Spirit of Christmas Past,"
said the ghost. "I have things to show you."

Together, they flew out of Scrooge's bedroom window
and into the cold night.

They soared up high above the smoky city, and flew into the
countryside. When Scrooge looked down there were children
playing in the snow, with adults helping to build snowmen.

As he hovered above them, he realized something.

"I know these people!" he said to the spirit. "Oh, I know them all from when I was a boy!"

Scrooge was surprised to find his heart swell with happiness at the sight of the familiar faces.

Next, the spirit took Scrooge to a school. In an empty classroom a lone boy sat with his books.

"Why, it's me!" cried Scrooge. "It's me as a boy."

A young woman entered the room, and he recognized his sister, Fan.

"I've persuaded Father to let me bring you home," said Fan.

Scrooge remembered how lonely he had felt that day, and how happy he had been to see his sister.

Finally, the spirit led Scrooge to a merry Christmas party.

Scrooge gasped when he saw himself as a young man, dancing with a pretty woman. "It's Belle," he said.

His heart ached as he remembered how Belle had broken off their engagement. Belle had said that Scrooge loved his money more than her.

He longed to stay, but the Spirit of Christmas Past said, "Come, Scrooge, it is time to take you home."

The spirit took Scrooge back to his room. Scrooge shivered, afraid of what might come next.

When the bells chimed once more, out of the gloom there came a merry figure dressed in green, smiling and holding out a hand.

"I am the Spirit of Christmas Present," she said. "Come, I have many things to show you."

And with that, she led Scrooge right out into the street. It was Christmas Day, and people were singing and laughing on their way to visit friends and relatives.

The spirit led Scrooge to Bob Cratchit's house.
Around the table sat Bob, his wife Mary, and their many
children. They didn't have much to eat or drink, but they
seemed happy.

"But what about that child?" Scrooge asked the spirit,
pointing to a small boy coughing into a handkerchief.

"That is Tiny Tim," said the spirit. "He is not well, but look how he smiles all the same."

Scrooge watched Tiny Tim closely. The family took such special care of the small boy and he had such a sweet nature, that Scrooge found himself moved to tears.

The spirit touched Scrooge's shoulder and led him away to the house of his nephew, Fred.

Fred and his wife were gathered with friends in their living room, playing such merry games that Scrooge himself laughed along with them — though they could not see nor hear him.

"A toast!" said Fred. "To Uncle Ebenezer! I shall always invite him for Christmas."

"Oh Fred," laughed his wife. "He will never come!"

"One day, he might. I wish he could enjoy himself!"

Scrooge felt a tug at his sleeve.

"Oh please, Spirit," he begged. "Let me watch this happy scene a little longer!"

"There is more to come, Scrooge," said the Spirit of Christmas Present. "I must take you home."

Back in his bedroom, a new spirit greeted Scrooge. This one was tall and cloaked in black and Scrooge was instantly afraid of him.

"I am the Spirit of Christmas Yet to Come," the ghost whispered.

He took Scrooge to a room where a laundress, a cleaner, and an undertaker were sorting through the belongings of a dead man.

"Let's sell it all, no one will know," the cleaner laughed.

"There is no one to miss this man, let alone his things!" agreed the others.

With a shudder, Scrooge recognized his own belongings. He was the dead man no one would miss!

"Spirit!" cried Scrooge. "Is there no grief?"

The spirit took Scrooge to the Cratchit house once more.

"There is grief," said the spirit. "Look."

Scrooge peered in through the window of the house. Inside, they were sewing black clothes and weeping. Bob Cratchit sat, forlorn, with his head in his hands.

They were mourning for Tiny Tim. The poor little boy had died.

Scrooge could bear no more. "Take me back," he begged.
"I have changed. Let me live again and try to chase away some
of these shadows that have yet to come."

And so the spirit led Scrooge back to his cold, bare room.

At last, Scrooge slept. When he awoke, it was daylight. He dressed quickly and ran outside, shouting out to a passing woman, "What day is it?"

"It is Christmas Day!" she answered with a laugh.

"I'm alive!" cried Scrooge. "Merry Christmas!" He shook her hand and gave her a coin.

He danced down the street, singing with joy.

He gave money to the people who were collecting for the poor.

He went into the butcher's. "I'll have your biggest turkey," he said. "Send it to the Cratchit family, please!"

"Oh spirits," he cried as he ran down the street. "Thank you! You have shown me the error of my ways. I will change!"

Scrooge went to his nephew Fred's house and asked
if he might still join them for dinner.

"Why, Uncle!" cried Fred. "Of course!"

He welcomed his uncle in for the merriest Christmas
either could remember.

The next day, when Bob Cratchit arrived for work nearly ten minutes late, Scrooge did not tell him off.

Instead, he gave him a pay raise, and promised thereafter to do whatever he could to help Bob and his family, especially Tiny Tim.

The spirits that visited Scrooge showed him what he had missed in the past, how he was missing the present, and what he might do to avoid a sad future.

Scrooge did change. He carried on giving to the poor and spending time with his family. He and Tiny Tim became friends who often shared in laughter at Christmas.

Scrooge had found joy and happiness in friends and family. And he never put money before love again.

Yes, Virginia, There Is a Santa Claus

Illustrated by Claire McElfatrick

More than 125 years ago, a little girl named Virginia O'Hanlon lived in New York City with her mother and father in a lovely home in a busy, bustling neighborhood. In those days, people rode in carriages or streetcars pulled by horses.

Virginia was eight years old and went to school to learn reading, writing, and arithmetic. She sat in a classroom with other children, wrote on a chalkboard, and practiced her printing and cursive with a feather-quill pen she dipped into an inkwell. Virginia was a curious and bright little girl, so when some of the older students were arguing whether or not Santa Claus was real, she hurried home to ask her father the truth.

"Papa, some of the children in my classroom believe Santa Claus is not real. Is it true?" Virginia asked with tears in her eyes.

Dr. O'Hanlon put down his newspaper and thought for a moment. He loved his little daughter and wanted her to be full of smiles. "I have an idea," he said. "I'll help you write a letter to the *Sun*." He tapped his newspaper. "If the *Sun* says there's a Santa Claus, it must be true."

Little Virginia did just that.

Dear Editor:

   I am 8 years old. Some of my little friends say there is no Santa Claus. Papa says "If you see it in The Sun it's so." Please tell me the truth; is there a Santa Claus?

Virginia O'Hanlon.
115 West Ninety-Fifth Street.

She wrote to the big, important New York newspaper, the *Sun*. Her letter landed on the desk of editor Francis Pharcellus Church.

Can you imagine the looks of happiness on the faces of Virginia and her family when they read the answer in the *Sun*? Well, that happiness quickly spread across the city, America, and the whole wide world. And this newspaper editorial by Mr. Church still brings tears of joy to our eyes today.

Virginia, your little friends are wrong. They have been affected by the skepticism of a skeptical age. They do not believe except they see. They think that nothing can be which is not comprehensible by their little minds. All minds, Virginia, whether they be men's or children's, are little. In this great universe of ours man is a mere insect, an ant, in his intellect, as compared with the boundless world about him, as measured by the intelligence capable of grasping the whole of truth and knowledge.

Yes, Virginia, there is a Santa Claus. He exists as certainly as love and generosity and devotion exist, and you know that they abound and give to your life its highest beauty and joy. Alas! how dreary would be the world if there were no Santa Claus. It would be as dreary as if there were no Virginias. There would be no childlike faith then, no poetry, no romance to make tolerable this existence. We should have no enjoyment, except in sense and sight. The eternal light with which childhood fills the world would be extinguished.

Not believe in Santa Claus! You might as well not believe in fairies! You might get your papa to hire men to watch in all the chimneys on Christmas Eve to catch Santa Claus, but even if they did not see Santa Claus coming down, what would that prove? Nobody sees Santa Claus, but that is no sign that there is no Santa Claus. The most real things in the world are those that neither children nor men can see. Did you ever see fairies dancing on the lawn? Of course not, but that's no proof that they are not there. Nobody can conceive or imagine all the wonders there are unseen and unseeable in the world.

You may tear apart the baby's rattle and see what makes the noise inside, but there is a veil covering the unseen world which not the strongest man, nor even the united strength of all the strongest men that ever lived, could tear apart. Only faith, fancy, poetry, love, romance, can push aside that curtain and view and picture the supernal beauty and glory beyond. Is it all real? Ah, Virginia, in all this world there is nothing else real and abiding.

No Santa Claus! Thank God! he lives, and he lives forever. A thousand years from now, Virginia, nay, ten times ten thousand years from now, he will continue to make glad the heart of childhood.

Jingle Bells

Dashing through the snow,
In a one-horse open sleigh,
O'er the fields we go,
Laughing all the way.
Bells on bobtails ring,
Making spirits bright.
What fun it is to ride and sing
A sleighing song tonight!

Oh, jingle bells, jingle bells,
Jingle all the way.
Oh, what fun it is to ride
In a one-horse open sleigh. Hey!
Jingle bells, jingle bells,
Jingle all the way!
Oh, what fun it is to ride
In a one-horse open sleigh.

Deck the Halls

Deck the halls with boughs of holly,
Fa la la la la, la la la la!
'Tis the season to be jolly,
Fa la la la la, la la la la!
Don we now our gay apparel,
Fa la la, la la la, la la la!
Troll the ancient Yuletide carol,
Fa la la la la, la la la la!

'Twas the Night
Before Christmas

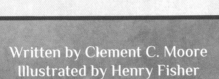

Written by Clement C. Moore
Illustrated by Henry Fisher

'Twas the night before Christmas,
when all through the house ...
Not a creature was stirring,
not even a mouse.

The stockings were hung
by the chimney with care,
in hopes that St. Nicholas
soon would be there.

The children were nestled all snug in their beds,
While visions of sugarplums danced in their heads.

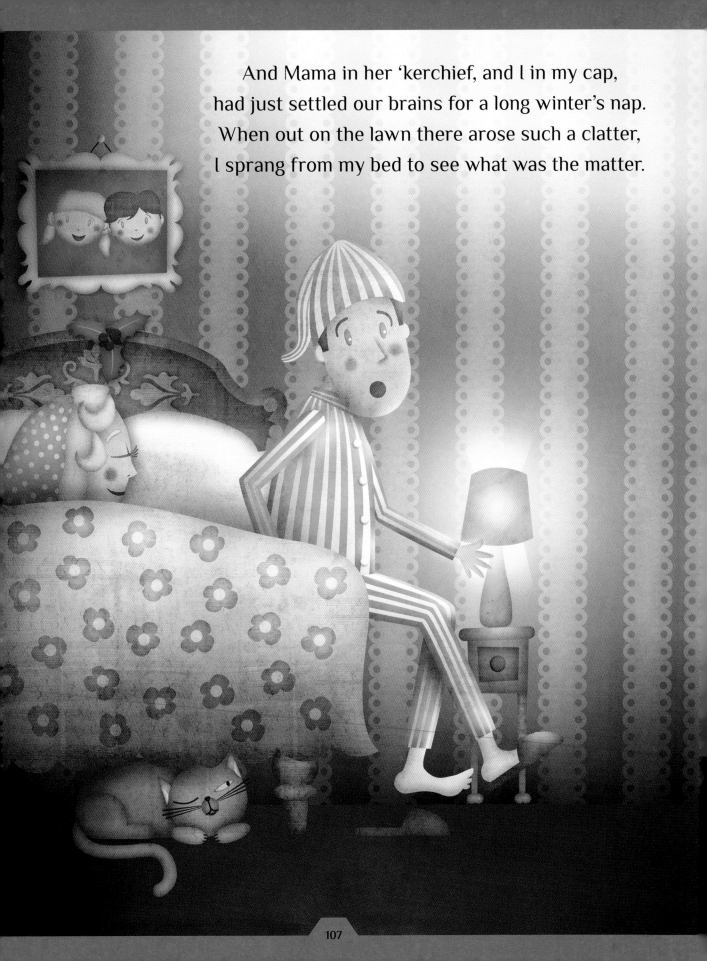

And Mama in her 'kerchief, and I in my cap,
had just settled our brains for a long winter's nap.
When out on the lawn there arose such a clatter,
I sprang from my bed to see what was the matter.

Away to the window l flew like a flash,
tore open the shutters and threw up the sash.
The moon on the breast of the new-fallen snow,
gave a lustre of midday to objects below.
When what to my wondering eyes did appear,
but a miniature sleigh and eight tiny reindeer.

With a little old driver so lively and quick,
I knew in a moment it must be St. Nick.

More rapid than eagles
his coursers they came,
and he whistled and shouted
and called them by name:

"Now, Dasher! Now, Dancer! Now, Prancer and Vixen!
On, Comet! On, Cupid! On, Donner and Blitzen!

"To the top of the porch! To the top of the wall!
Now dash away! Dash away! Dash away all!"

As leaves that before the wild hurricane fly,
when they meet with an obstacle, mount to the sky.
So up to the housetop the coursers they flew,
with a sleigh full of toys, and St. Nicholas, too —

And then, in a twinkling, I heard on the roof
the prancing and pawing of each little hoof.

As I drew in my head, and was turning around,
down the chimney St. Nicholas came with a bound.

He was dressed all in fur, from his head to his foot
and his clothes were all tarnished with ashes and soot.
A bundle of toys he had flung on his back,
and he looked like a peddler just opening his pack.

His eyes—how they twinkled!
His dimples—how merry!
His cheeks were like roses, his nose like a cherry!
His droll little mouth was drawn up like a bow,
and the beard on his chin was as white as the snow.

He had a broad face
and a little round belly
that shook when he laughed,
like a bowl full of jelly.

He was chubby and plump, a right jolly old elf,
and I laughed when I saw him, in spite of myself.
A wink of his eye and a twist of his head
soon gave me to know I had nothing to dread.

He spoke not a word, but went straight to his work,
and filled all the stockings, then turned with a jerk.

And laying his finger aside of his nose,
and giving a nod, up the chimney he rose.

He sprang to his sleigh, to his team gave a whistle,
and away they all flew like the down of a thistle.
But I heard him exclaim, ere he drove out of sight —
"Happy Christmas to all, and to all a goodnight!"

The First Noel

The first Noel, the angels did say
Was to certain poor shepherds in fields as they lay.
In fields where they lay, keeping their sheep,
On a cold winter's night that was so deep.

Noel, Noel, Noel, Noel
Born is the King of Israel!

Good King Wenceslas

Good King Wenceslas looked out,
On the Feast of Stephen,
When the snow lay round about,
Deep and crisp and even;
Brightly shone the moon that night,
Though the frost was cruel,
When a poor man came in sight,
Gath'ring winter fuel.

Things You Never Knew about Santa Claus

Written by Giles Paley-Phillips
Illustrated by Rowan Martin

Way up in the cold North Pole,
far, far away from you,

Santa Claus is doing things
you won't believe are true!

Did you know that Mr. Claus
sunbathes in the snow?
THAT's why he has such rosy cheeks —
I bet you didn't know!

He does of course have reindeer,
like all the stories say,
but he also has ...

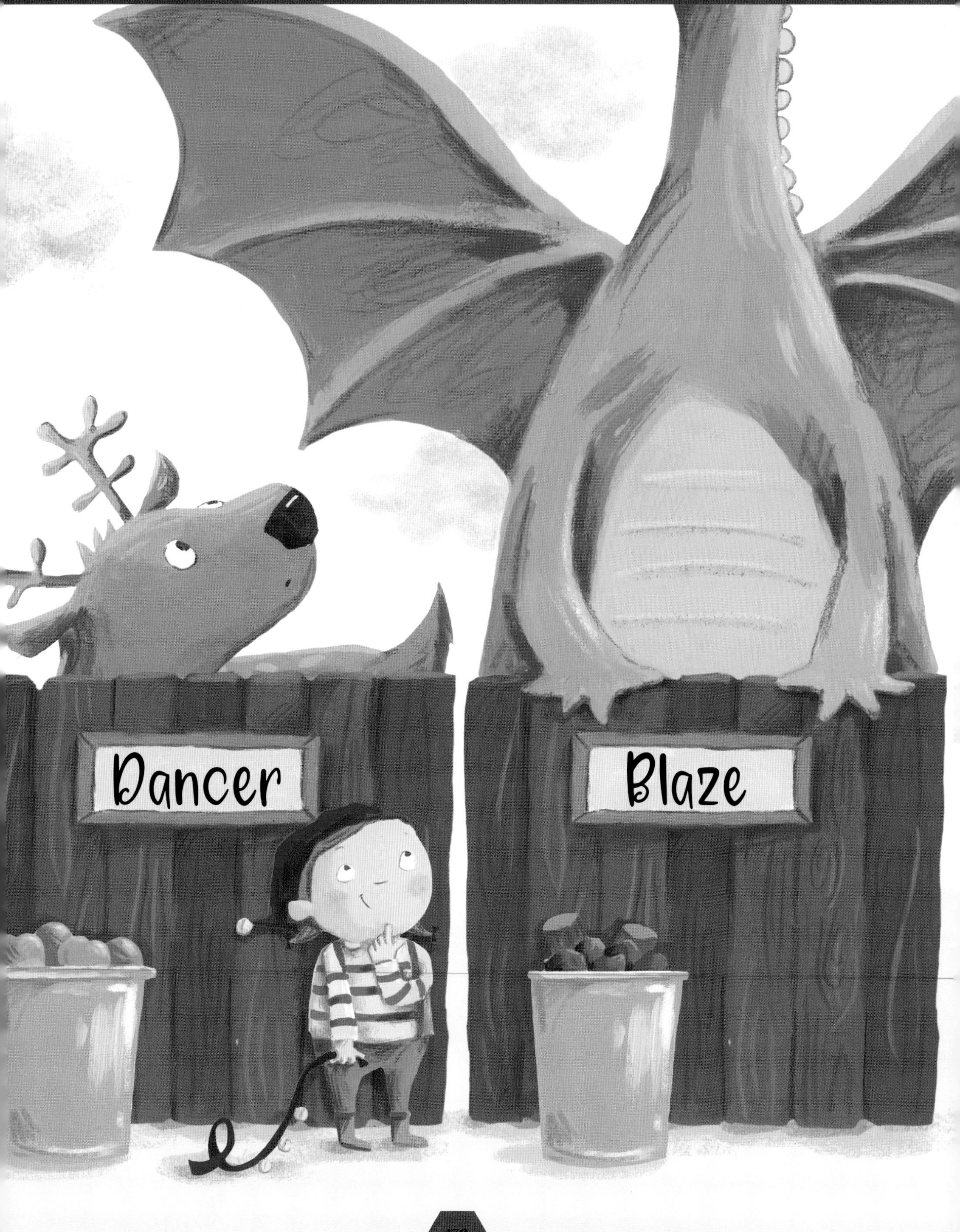
Dancer
Blaze

...a dragon that he rides on every day!

One thing we all know
is that Santa loves to eat,
but did you know ...

...COLD PIZZA is his favorite midnight treat?

Santa Claus loves bumper cars and chasing reindeer around.

When he's tired of jingle bells,
he likes a

HARD ROCK SOUND!

Santa likes to dye his hair,
which makes him look quite weird.
Would you believe his latest look?

A green and purple beard!

On Christmas Eve he goes by sleigh,
but Santa loves to SCOOT!
Then he wears his bright blue shorts
and not his crimson suit.

Sharing gifts around the world,
he's never lost his way.
But sometimes Santa *does* get lost—
when he takes some time away!

SANTA'S COMING...

Yes, Santa Claus does lots of things,

it's all COMPLETELY true!
but the thing he likes to do the most...

...is bring some joy to you!

We Three Kings

We three kings of Orient are,
Bearing gifts we traverse afar,
Field and fountain, moor and mountain,
Following yonder star.

O star of wonder, star of night,
Star with royal beauty bright,
Westward leading, still proceeding,
Guide us to thy perfect light.

O Little Town of Bethlehem

O little town of Bethlehem,
How still we see thee lie!
Above thy deep and dreamless sleep
The silent stars go by;
Yet in thy dark streets shineth
The everlasting light.
The hopes and fears of all the years
Are met in thee tonight.

The Twelve Days of Christmas

Illustrated by
Victoria Assanelli

On the first day of Christmas
my true love gave to me
a partridge in a pear tree.

On the second day of Christmas
my true love gave to me
two turtle doves,

and a partridge in a pear tree.

On the third day of Christmas
my true love gave to me
three French hens,
two turtle doves,
and a partridge in a pear tree.

On the fourth day of Christmas
my true love gave to me
four calling birds,

three French hens,
two turtle doves,
and a partridge in a pear tree.

On the fifth day of Christmas
my true love gave to me

five golden rings,

four calling birds,
three French hens,
two turtle doves,
and a partridge in a pear tree.

On the sixth day of Christmas
my true love gave to me
six geese a-laying,

five golden rings,
four calling birds,
three French hens,
two turtle doves,
and a partridge in a pear tree.

On the seventh day of Christmas
my true love gave to me
seven swans a-swimming,

six geese a-laying,
five golden rings,
four calling birds,
three French hens,
two turtle doves,
and a partridge in a pear tree.

On the eighth day of Christmas
my true love gave to me
eight maids a-milking,

seven swans a-swimming,
six geese a-laying,
five golden rings,
four calling birds,
three French hens,
two turtle doves,
and a partridge in a pear tree.

On the ninth day of Christmas
my true love gave to me
nine ladies dancing,

eight maids a-milking,
seven swans a-swimming,
six geese a-laying,
five golden rings,
four calling birds,
three French hens,
two turtle doves,
and a partridge in a pear tree.

On the tenth day of Christmas
my true love gave to me
ten lords a-leaping,

nine ladies dancing,
eight maids a-milking,
seven swans a-swimming,
six geese a-laying,
five golden rings,
four calling birds,
three French hens,
two turtle doves,
and a partridge in a pear tree.

On the eleventh day of Christmas
my true love gave to me
eleven pipers piping,

ten lords a-leaping,
nine ladies dancing,
eight maids a-milking,
seven swans a-swimming,
six geese a-laying,
five golden rings,
four calling birds,
three French hens,
two turtle doves,
and a partridge in a pear tree.

On the twelfth day of Christmas
my true love gave to me
twelve drummers drumming,

eleven pipers piping,
ten lords a-leaping,
nine ladies dancing,
eight maids a-milking,
seven swans a-swimming,
six geese a-laying,
five golden rings,
four calling birds,
three French hens,
two turtle doves,
and a partridge in a pear tree!

Silent Night

Silent night, holy night
All is calm, all is bright.
'Round yon Virgin, Mother and Child,
Holy Infant so tender and mild.
Sleep in heavenly peace.
Sleep in heavenly peace.

We Wish You a Merry Christmas

We wish you a merry Christmas,
We wish you a merry Christmas,
We wish you a merry Christmas,
And a happy New Year.

Good tidings we bring
To you and your kin.
We wish you a merry Christmas,
And a happy New Year!